D0312967

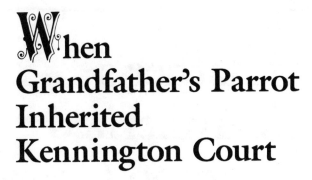

When Grandfather's Parrot Inherited Kennington Court

When Grandfather's Parrot Inherited Kennington Court

by Linda Allen

*Illustrated by
Katinka Kew*

Little, Brown and Company
Boston   Toronto   London

Text copyright © 1988 by Linda Allen

Illustrations copyright © 1988 by Hodder and Stoughton Ltd.

First U.S. Edition 1990

The characters and events in this book are fictitious. Any similarity to
real persons, living or dead, is coincidental and not intended by the
author.

First published in the U.K. in 1988 by Hodder and Stoughton Ltd.

Library of Congress Cataloging-in-Publication Data

Allen, Linda.
    When Grandfather's parrot inherited Kennington Court/by Linda
Allen; illustrated by Katinka Kew.
        p.   cm.
    Previously published under title: A parrot in the house.
    Summary: Appalled that Grandfather left his inheritance to his parrot,
the relatives seek to break the will; but young Miranda, who is caring
for the parrot, makes a discovery that settles everything.
    ISBN 0-316-03413-4
    [1. Mystery and detective stories. 2. Parrots — Fiction. 3. En-
gland — Fiction.] I. Kew, Katinka, ill. II. Allen, Linda. Parrot in
the house. III. Title.
PZ7.A4277Wh   1990
[Fic] — dc20   89-13282
                                                              CIP
                                                               AC

Joy Street Books are published by Little, Brown and Company (Inc.).

10 9 8 7 6 5 4 3 2 1
BP
Published simultaneously in Canada
by Little, Brown & Company (Canada) Limited

PRINTED IN THE UNITED STATES OF AMERICA

Contents

When Grandfather's Parrot Inherited Kennington Court

⌐Chapter 1
The Reading of the Will

What?" roared Uncle Fennimore.

"It isn't legal to bequeath a house to a parrot," shouted Cousin Horace.

"I'm afraid it is," sighed Mr. Fulton, the lawyer.

Miranda came out of her daydream and looked at Aunt Lucille. "What's the matter?" she asked. "Why is everybody so angry?"

"Because Grandfather Kennington left Kennington Court to his pet parrot," said Aunt Lucille.

"Why are they angry about that?" asked Miranda.

"I can't imagine," Aunt Lucille replied. "It seems perfectly reasonable to me."

"Horace," snapped Aunt Dorothy, who was married to Uncle Fennimore, "look after your mother. She appears to have fainted."

3

Miranda looked across the room at Aunt Jane, who was lying on a sofa with her mouth open and her wig all crooked. Cousin Horace bent over her and yelled, "Mother, wake up!"

Aunt Jane gave a little moan. "What's the matter?" she asked. "Where am I?" Aunt Jane had once been an actress and she could faint beautifully.

"You're at Kennington Court, Mother. You're here for the will-reading."

"Oh, it isn't true — tell me it isn't true!"

"Of course it's true, Mother. Isn't it just the sort of thing he would do? I always said the old boy was as mad as a hatter."

Aunt Dorothy said, "Well, I think it's ridiculous. A parrot can't pay the household bills and give the housekeeper instructions."

Then Mrs. Bloomers, the housekeeper, interrupted to ask what *her* position was, now that the

house belonged to a parrot. Mr. Fulton said it was exactly as it had always been. She was to stay on as housekeeper.

"How can I take orders from a parrot?" she demanded. "I'm allergic to parrots. They make me sneeze."

Aunt Lucille gave a little snort and clapped her handkerchief to her mouth. Her eyes were watering and her shoulders were shaking with laughter. Miranda couldn't help giggling at the thought of Mrs. Bloomers asking the parrot what she ought to prepare for dinner.

Mr. Fulton said, "If I could have your attention, everybody . . ."

Miranda listened carefully. She had thought the will-reading was going to be boring, but now it was getting quite interesting. She wondered where the parrot was.

"Under the terms of the will," Mr. Fulton was saying, "you are all entitled to use the house as a holiday home, but in return for this privilege you will be expected to take care of the bird. Mr. Kennington left a full list of duties regarding his welfare — that is, the parrot's welfare — which you are advised to study carefully."

Mrs. Bloomers asked who was to do the cooking and cleaning if all these people were going to stay at once. So far Aunt Grace hadn't said much, but she glared at Mrs. Bloomers and called her an impertinent woman.

"I think I may venture to suggest, Mrs. Bloomers," put in Mr. Fulton, "that you will overcome these difficulties in time. I shall be coming to the house quite regularly to make sure that all is going

smoothly, and if there are any problems I am sure we shall be able to sort them out."

Cousin Horace suddenly said, "Well, it doesn't sound too bad. If we can all use the house it means that it belongs to all of us."

"What good is that?" snapped Uncle Fennimore. "We shall never know who is the real master of the house."

"The parrot is," said Miranda, but nobody took any notice of her.

Aunt Lucille was trying to stop laughing. She wiped her eyes. "Has anybody *told* the parrot yet?" she inquired.

"Really, Lucille," said Aunt Grace, "I fail to see what you find so amusing in all this. Don't pretend you weren't hoping that Kennington Court had been left to you."

"It never crossed my mind," said Aunt Lucille. "Poor relations don't inherit English manor houses."

"Come off it," sneered Cousin Horace. "We all wanted the house. Grandfather Kennington knew that, and that's why he did this — to make fools of us."

"Oh, I'm sure you're being a little unfair," responded Aunt Lucille. "You know how he adored birds. They were his whole life. He never made any secret of the fact that he preferred them to human beings. In fact, birds, to him, *were* people, and I think that is a point of view we should respect. I feel the same way about donkeys."

"You know, Lucille," said Aunt Grace, "I am beginning to have very serious doubts about your being a suitable guardian for that child." She always referred to Miranda as *that child*. "If that's the sort of nonsense you are putting into her head, then it's high time she went to boarding school."

"I couldn't afford it," said Aunt Lucille cheerfully. She reached out her hand and took Miranda's, as if to reassure her that she would never, under any circumstances, send her away. Aunt Lucille was poor, although the rest of the family was rich, yet it had been Aunt Lucille who had wanted to adopt Miranda when her parents had died. They lived in a tiny house on a shabby street, and their relatives never visited them there, but Miranda and Aunt Lucille occasionally went to visit them in their own homes.

"Oh, well," said Aunt Grace, "I suppose you're making the best of things, but I know quite well you'd have loved to inherit this house."

"Well, of course I would," said Aunt Lucille, "and if I had, I would have bought some donkeys. Lots of donkeys."

"May I speak?" said Mr. Fulton. Everybody looked at him again, and he went on, "You will no doubt have realized that it is in your own interests to ensure that the parrot is well taken care of. As long as he lives you will all be able to enjoy the comforts of this beautiful old house."

"As long as he lives?" repeated Cousin Horace. "Why — what happens when he snuffs it?"

Miranda glared at him.

"I shall be coming to that later," said Mr. Fulton. "When Mr. Kennington was taken ill, the parrot was put in the care of a local vet — Mr. Ryman. Strictly speaking, I should have waited for Mr. Ryman to arrive with the bird before I commenced proceedings, but he was unfortunately delayed at the last moment and telephoned to say he would be here as soon as possible."

"I'll go and wait for him," said Miranda. She slipped out of the French windows onto the terrace, where she sat down on the balustrade, swinging her legs. She thought about Grandfather Kennington. He had really been her great-grandfather. When her parents had died she had been brought to see him, and he had been very kind, but that was a long time ago. Then, when Aunt Lucille had adopted her, he had sent for her again. He had tried to persuade Aunt Lucille to take money from him, but Aunt Lucille had refused. She had said she wanted to bring up Miranda as if she were her own child, and that meant providing for her herself. They were by no means well-off, but they were happy, and Miranda wouldn't have lived with anybody else, however much money that person had.

About a year ago Grandfather Kennington had invited all his relations to tea. It was such an unusual occurrence that they had wondered why, but he hadn't explained. He had talked to them about birds. Miranda had found it most interesting, but Cousin Horace had been very rude. "He's quite mad, you know," he had said when Grandfather Kennington was out of the way, "bringing us all here to give us a lecture on birds. As if any of us cared two hoots about hedge sparrows or wagtails or . . ."

"Or owls." Aunt Lucille had smiled, but only Miranda had understood the little joke.

After tea they had walked about the grounds. Grandfather Kennington had wanted them to see the nest boxes he had had put up in the trees. Everyone except Miranda and Aunt Lucille had been bored after a while and had gone back indoors to rest. That was when Grandfather Kennington had taken them down to the lake and pointed out the platform that he had made for the swans on the island. Coming back through the shrubbery he had told Miranda where the robins' nest was. There were young birds in the nest, he had told her. He knew that because he had watched the parent birds taking food to them. But when Miranda had asked if she could peep at them he had said, "Certainly not — how would you like it if people came to

stare at you when you were in bed?" That was
what Aunt Lucille had meant when she had said
that Grandfather Kennington looked upon birds
as people. They had as much right to be treated
with respect as human beings had. Miranda understood that now.

Suddenly a little square car appeared and pulled
up beside the other cars belonging to Miranda's
uncles and aunts. She couldn't help smiling at the
contrast — Uncle Fennimore and Aunt Dorothy's
elegant car with its huge headlights and shining
brasswork; Cousin Horace's sports model with the
folding top; Aunt Grace's chauffeur-driven lim-
ousine (as she insisted on calling it). Beside them,
the little Morris Ten looked as chirpy and cheerful
as a fat old hen.

Mr. Ryman, the vet, got out and then took out a huge birdcage containing a bright green parrot. Miranda jumped down off the balustrade and went to meet him. "Hello," she said.

"Hello. Who are you?"

"I'm Miranda."

"Jim Ryman." They shook hands. "I'm afraid I'm rather late. I had to call and see a sick goat. Has anything interesting happened yet?"

"Yes," Miranda said, "the parrot has inherited Kennington Court."

Mr. Ryman's mouth dropped open, then it turned up in a delighted grin. "I must admit I'm rather glad to hear it," he said.

"So am I," said Miranda. She liked Mr. Ryman already.

As they walked along the terrace toward the open French windows, she asked, "What's the parrot's name?"

"Carey."

"Welcome home, Carey," she said.

Chapter 2
The Mysterious Box

Carey's appearance was met with hostile silence. Mr. Ryman said, "Good morning," but only Aunt Lucille returned the greeting. The others glared at him as if by bringing the parrot into the house he was the cause of all their grievances. He placed the cage on a small table and took a seat nearby. Miranda joined him. She began to talk softly to the bird.

"Have you got a pet of your own?" Mr. Ryman asked.

"No. I live with Aunt Lucille. That's Aunt Lucille over there. She has to go to work every day and it wouldn't be right to leave a pet in the house all alone."

"Quite right," said Mr. Ryman, staring across the room at Aunt Lucille.

Uncle Fennimore said in a loud voice, "Can we get on with it? We've already been kept waiting long enough."

"Well, now," said Mr. Fulton, "I think we should explain to Mr. Ryman what has already been said."

"About Carey's inheritance?" said Mr. Ryman. "There's no need to go over all that — Miranda told me."

"Oh, she did, did she?" Cousin Horace burst out. "Cheeky little blighter."

Miranda glared at him. He was only nineteen himself and he often behaved like a spoiled little boy.

"Does the parrot talk?" inquired Aunt Dorothy.

"Talk?" said Mrs. Bloomers. "It can talk the hind leg off a donkey when it starts. You'd never believe the silly nonsense it's been taught to say."

"Mr. Ryman," said Aunt Lucille innocently, "is it, in your opinion as a vet, really possible for a parrot to talk the hind leg off a donkey? I only ask because I am partial to donkeys."

Aunt Grace said, "Is it all right for that child to be so close to the bird? Isn't there some dreadful disease that parrots can pass on to human beings?"

Mr. Ryman, who was laughing at what Aunt Lucille had said, turned to Aunt Grace. "I assure you," he said, "that Carey is in perfect health."

Cousin Horace's eyes gleamed. He leaned forward toward Mr. Fulton. "What happens when the parrot snuffs it?" he asked.

There was a deathly silence. Miranda broke it. "You might have waited till Carey was out of the room before you asked that," she said.

"I have been trying to explain," said Mr. Fulton (which wasn't quite right, because all he had succeeded in doing since Mr. Ryman came into the room was open his mouth and shut it again), "I have been trying to explain that when that unfortunate event takes place, the property will go to charity."

"Jane's going off again," said Uncle Fennimore.

"Mother," roared Cousin Horace, "buck up, old girl!"

"Unless . . ." shouted Mr. Fulton, and once again there was complete silence. Carey scratched himself nonchalantly. "Unless one of you should prove worthy to inherit the property," finished Mr. Fulton.

"What on earth do you mean by that?" asked Aunt Dorothy.

"Worthy in what way?" shouted Uncle Fennimore.

"Quite frankly," said Mr. Fulton, "I don't know."

"But you're the lawyer," said Cousin Horace. "You ought to know."

Mr. Fulton drew their attention to a small metal box that had been lying on the desk in front of him ever since the will-reading had begun. "Before the late Mr. Kennington was taken ill," he said, "he sent for me and handed me this box. I, of course, was aware of the terms of his will, but it seems that Mr. Kennington had some second thoughts. The will, however, is to stand until someone — one of you here in the room today — presents me with the key to this box."

"Well?" said Uncle Fennimore impatiently. "Go on."

"That's all," said Mr. Fulton.

"All? What do you mean — all? You must know more than that."

"I'm afraid I don't."

Everybody started talking at once.

"Who's got the key?"

"What's in the box?"

"The whole thing must be contested."

"You must know what the box contains."

It was Aunt Lucille who brought them all to order by ringing a little bell she found on the mantelpiece. "Thank you, Mr. Fulton," she said. "As I understand it, the whole of the property belongs to Carey for his lifetime, unless one of us presents the key to that box. And we can only obtain the key by somehow proving worthy to inherit in Carey's place. Is that it?"

Mr. Fulton nodded. "Exactly."

Cousin Horace became excited. "It's a treasure hunt!" he yelled. "Grandfather Kennington hid the key somewhere in this house and whoever is clever enough to work out where it might be hidden is a suitable person — worthy to inherit the place."

"Oh, how quick you are, dear," said Aunt Jane. "You must be right."

"Of course I'm right. And I shall turn this house upside down until I find that key."

"Oh no you won't," said Mrs. Bloomers firmly.

Mr. Ryman stood up. "I have to release Carey into the conservatory," he said. "Those were my instructions. Coming, Miranda?"

Miranda would never forget the sight of Carey coming out of his cage and flying around the conservatory. He was so glad to be home. "I never

saw him before," she said to Mr. Ryman. "Grandfather Kennington told me he had a parrot in his conservatory, but I didn't know whether to believe him or not."

"He's a very fine bird," Mr. Ryman said; and then, "I like your Aunt Lucille. It must be fun living with her."

"It is," said Miranda.

"Does anyone else live with you?" asked Mr. Ryman.

"No. Uncle Rob was killed in the war."

"What happened to your parents?"

"They died."

"I'm sorry. Maybe I shouldn't have asked."

"That's all right. Aunt Lucille is my mother's sister. I don't care about the others, Aunt Dorothy and Uncle Fennimore and Cousin Horace, and Aunt Jane and Aunt Grace. I'm glad it was Aunt Lucille who adopted me."

"So am I. Shall we get back to them? Mr. Fulton is anxious to get away."

There was very little more to be said. Mr. Fulton reminded them that it was in their interests to take good care of the parrot until the key to the box was found. "For remember," he said, "if the bird should die before the key is found, the property goes to charity."

"You'll take care of him, Ryman, won't you?" said Uncle Fennimore, clapping Mr. Ryman on the shoulder. "Fulton tells me you've been retained to pay him a weekly visit. We'll — er — we'll come to some arrangement when the key turns up. Just make sure the bird's in tip-top condition, eh?"

Mr. Ryman made no answer. Mr. Fulton said, "Here is the list of duties regarding the daily welfare of the bird. Mr. Kennington was most anxious that it should be followed very conscientiously."

Glancing at the list, Aunt Dorothy said, "This is ridiculous. I never saw such nonsense. Well, I

for one am not prepared to go to such lengths, just for the sake of a parrot."

"Don't expect me to do *anything* for it," said Aunt Jane. "I can't stand birds. I can't bear the way they flutter their wings."

"I'll look after him," said Miranda.

"That's a good girl," said Aunt Dorothy. "Here — you take the list and do what you can."

Mr. Fulton went out. Uncle Fennimore and Aunt Dorothy started whispering together. Aunt Grace was having an argument with Mrs. Bloomers about lunch, and Cousin Horace was trying to open one of the drawers in the desk without anybody seeing him. Aunt Jane was pretending to weep. And Aunt Lucille accompanied Mr. Ryman to his car.

Miranda took the list into the conservatory. She studied it carefully, then she looked up to the high perch on which Carey was sitting.

"Grandfather Kennington says here that you must get accustomed to my voice," she said, "that is, the person who has undertaken to feed you and look after you. Did you know that he left this house to you — the furniture and the pictures and everything? I'm very pleased. I think you're beautiful."

Carey shuffled about from one foot to the other, but he didn't say anything.

"I'm supposed to call you 'good old Carey' and say 'come to Pop' when it's time for your food. But that's not quite yet. And I'm supposed to wear Grandfather Kennington's old hat when I give you your dinner. I suppose that's it, hanging behind the door. And there's a glove in the drawer by the sink and seed in the barrel, and a special brush for your cage. Grandfather Kennington thought of everything."

She went on talking to him for a long time until she heard the bell for lunch; then she went out quietly, closing the door behind her.

Chapter 3
Carey Speaks

After lunch Miranda hurried back to the conservatory. Everybody had been talking about the key to the box. That had given Miranda an idea, but she didn't want to tell anybody about it yet — not even Aunt Lucille.

Carey was perched on the grapevine. He looked at Miranda with his head on one side. "Hello, Carey," she said.

"Hello," he replied.

Miranda was speechless with excitement. Her heart was thumping. She had never heard a bird speak before. It was a strange sound that seemed to come from deep in his throat, and though he couldn't pronounce the "l" properly there was no doubt that he had imitated the word very cleverly. They went on saying hello to each other for quite a long time, until the door opened and Uncle Fennimore and Aunt Dorothy came in.

"Well, Miranda," said Uncle Fennimore, "how are you getting on with the bird? Jolly good, jolly good," he said without waiting for her to reply. "Keep it up and you shall have half-a-crown for Christmas. Where is he? Oh, I see him. Has he said anything yet?"

"Not much."

"This place is like a jungle," put in Aunt Dorothy. "We must get Simmonds the gardener to trim it all back."

"You can't do that," said Miranda.

"My dear child, you mustn't contradict your elders. Hasn't your Aunt Lucille taught you *anything* about good manners?"

"Yes," said Miranda, "she told me that adults are far more rude than children are."

"*Well!* Did you hear that, Fennimore? I think you ought to have a word with Lucille."

"You can't trim the plants in here," said Miranda doggedly, "because it says so in the list."

"What?" cried Aunt Dorothy in an unbelieving tone of voice.

"All these plants were specially grown for a parrot," Miranda went on. "Simmonds knows when to prune them — that's what the list says — and if anybody — I forget what the word was — but if you don't do as it says in the list, Mr. Fulton has to be informed."

Aunt Dorothy glared at Miranda as if she would like to bite her. "Quite unbelievable!" she shouted. "I think we ought to contest the will on the grounds that Grandfather Kennington was of unsound mind."

"I had a word with Fulton about that," said Uncle Fennimore. "He says the old boy had enclosed a document with the will certifying that he was *compos mentis*." Miranda didn't know what that meant, but it seemed to annoy Aunt Dorothy, so she smiled to herself.

Aunt Dorothy said, "Simmonds has enough to do outside without having to water all these plants every day."

"He doesn't have to," Miranda told her. "There's a sprinkler."

"A what?"

"A sprinkler. You turn it on down here. It says so in the list."

"That stupid list . . ." began Aunt Dorothy, but Miranda had already turned the wheel and the sprinkler came on. Aunt Dorothy gave a little shriek and tried to cover her hair with her hands. She was always worrying about her hair. "Turn it off!" she shouted.

"I can't," said Miranda, "it's stuck."

Aunt Dorothy and Uncle Fennimore hurried out. "Hello," chuckled Carey, "hello, hello."

Miranda burst out laughing. She could almost believe that he understood. It was now time for his dinner, so she put on Grandfather Kennington's old hat and, in accordance with the instructions, ran a pencil back and forth across the bars of his cage, making a rattling sound. Carey began to get excited. She called, "Dinnertime, Carey. Good boy, come to Pop."

"Hello," he responded, "good boy," and then, to her amazement, "truly thankful."

She held her breath for a moment. She remembered that Grandfather Kennington had always insisted on grace being said before every meal. Was

it possible that he had said it even at Carey's dinnertime? As she put out his meal of chopped fruit, nuts, and seeds, she said as calmly as she could, "For what we are about to receive may the Lord make us . . ."

There was a whirr of wings, a draft of air just above her ear, and Carey popped into his cage. "Truly thankful," he said, and began to gobble.

"Oh, Carey," she said, "what a wonderful bird you are! What else did Grandfather Kennington teach you to do, I wonder." She was still musing on this thought when Cousin Horace came in.

"I want to talk to you," he said.

"What about?"

"About the day when we all came to tea with Grandfather Kennington. Can you remember what he talked about?"

"He talked about lots of things." She wished he would go. She wanted to have Carey to herself again. She knew she was making good progress with him.

"Such as?" asked Cousin Horace.

"The weather. Scotland. People who ate too much."

"No, what I mean is, did he say anything in particular to you? You seemed to be pretty pally when you were in the garden."

A wicked little plan for getting rid of him entered her head. "He talked about birds' nests," she said, quite truthfully. "He told me that I ought not to look into birds' nests when there were young birds in them. He said they could be aggressive at that time of the year. Especially magpies." She glanced innocently into Cousin Horace's face. "Did you know that magpies love shiny objects? They pick them up and take them back to their nests."

His eyes gleamed. "Good girl," he said. "Anything else?"

She turned away from him and said over her shoulder, "Only about the cellars. He used to play down there when he was a little boy. He used to hide his special treasures in the wine cellar. He said it was the best hiding place he'd ever had."

Cousin Horace gave a sort of whoop and rumpled her hair. "Thanks, Miranda," he said as he hurried out.

Carey was still pecking at his food. Miranda sat down on a stool with her chin on her hand, watching him. She talked softly to him, saying anything that came into her mind. It was very important to make him feel at ease with her, not only because of the idea that was buzzing around in her head, but because Grandfather Kennington had loved

him and had wanted somebody else to care for him, too.

She did not even turn when someone came into the conservatory. She was in one of her daydreams again.

"Good heavens, Miranda!" Aunt Grace said. "What are you doing wearing Grandfather Kennington's old hat? You gave me quite a start."

"I have to wear it when I give Carey his dinner,"

replied Miranda dreamily. "It says so in the list."

"Oh, you mustn't attach too much importance to that list," said Aunt Grace. "It's quite obviously a practical joke."

"No, it isn't," Miranda said, without even thinking that she was contradicting an adult again. "It works. I did everything that was in the list and Carey spoke to me. He said grace."

Aunt Grace gave a little laugh. "Why, how sweet of Grandfather Kennington to teach his pet to say my name!" she cried. "But then, I always felt that he had a special regard for me."

"I didn't mean . . ." began Miranda, but Aunt Grace didn't seem to hear her.

"And I was always so attentive to him, pouring his tea first and making sure that he didn't feel the draft, and I never failed to send him a Christmas card, so it's no wonder that he spoke about me in my absence — even if it was only to the parrot. . . ."

"Did you want something?" Miranda asked.

"I beg your pardon?"

"Did you come to see me about something?"

"Oh — no — I saw Horace sneaking in here in a furtive sort of way and I wondered what he was up to."

"He was here," said Miranda, "but he went out. He went to look at the wine cellar."

"I wonder why," murmured Aunt Grace.

"I think it might have been because I told him about Grandfather Kennington hiding his treasures in there when he was a little boy."

"Now, how on earth did you know that?"

"Grandfather Kennington told me himself."

Aunt Grace's eyes gleamed and she went out.

"Now, Carey," said Miranda, "where were we?"

Chapter 4
Aunt Lucille Goes to Town

At breakfast the next morning Aunt Lucille said, "It's market day today. I have to go into town to do some shopping. Will you take me, Horace?"

"I'm going to be busy all day," he replied, "but Mother will drive you in."

"I couldn't *possibly*," said Aunt Jane, who was still in her frilly pink dressing gown, "not on market day. All those animals and people — and besides, Lucille, there are no dress shops worth looking at. Why not leave it until tomorrow?"

"I'm sorry," Aunt Lucille answered patiently, "we're out of food supplies and if I don't go shopping nobody will eat tonight."

"No food!" exclaimed Uncle Fennimore. "What is that woman Bloomers doing to run out of supplies?"

43

"I knew this silly business wouldn't work," broke in Aunt Dorothy. "As I said yesterday, *somebody* has to be in charge here. It's all very well saying the parrot owns the house, but how can a parrot order bread and vegetables and all the other things we need?"

"That's why I'm going into town," explained Aunt Lucille.

"I wasn't aware," Aunt Dorothy went on, "that we had voted you in charge of the running of the house, Lucille."

Miranda put her hand over her mouth so she wouldn't cry out that nobody but Aunt Lucille had done anything to help Mrs. Bloomers and Kitty in the kitchen; nobody had thought about making up all the beds yesterday afternoon; and nobody had offered to help with Carey. They were all sitting there expecting things to be done for them as if by magic.

Aunt Grace said, "Is that child going to be sick? Why has she got her hand over her mouth? Why is she staring at me like that?" She was still furious with Miranda because she had gotten herself locked in the wine cellar yesterday, though Miranda couldn't understand why she should be. After all, she had only answered Aunt Grace's questions about Horace. As for Cousin Horace himself, he had bumped into the cellar door and still had a sore red nose for his trouble. Well, thought Miranda, I can't be popular with everybody all the time. At least Carey likes me.

"What about lending me your car, Aunt Grace?" asked Aunt Lucille. "I'm sure Howson won't mind driving me in."

"*My* car? To carry potatoes and cabbages and goodness knows what else besides? I couldn't allow that. Do be reasonable, Lucille."

Miranda spoke up. "It's all right, Aunt Lucille," she said, "Mr. Ryman is coming at half past nine to bring some vitamin pills for Carey. He won't mind giving you a ride in his car. He won't mind what his car smells of. And I'm sure he'll bring you back again, because he likes you."

"Does he indeed?" Aunt Dorothy sniffed, but Aunt Lucille only smiled and said that was all right, then.

Later, when everybody had finished breakfast and Aunt Lucille had gone into town with Mr. Ryman, Miranda went to give Carey his fresh water. She had just done that when the door at the end of the conservatory opened and an old man came in.

" 'Morning, miss," he said, touching his cap. "Perkins the odd-job man. Is the master around?"

Miranda glanced up at Carey, then she said, "If you mean my great-grandfather Kennington, he died."

"Yes, miss, I knows that," he said and, as if recollecting something, took off his cap, "but I reckons as there must be a new master here now. I comes in regular once a month to do any odd jobs as needs doing."

Miranda said, "Well, I don't know. You see, Grandfather Kennington left all his property to the parrot, so he must be the new master."

"You're pulling my leg, miss, just 'cause I'm an old man, and that's not kind."

"I'm not pulling your leg," said Miranda. "It's quite true."

The old man gazed at her, and when he saw that she was serious he cackled in delight. "Oh, that's a good 'un, that is! Oh, just like old master, that is. Yes, he'd do that, he would." And so he went on, stopping every now and then only to look up at Carey, until Uncle Fennimore came in.

"Who's this?" Uncle Fennimore said.

"Perkins, odd jobs. Once a month," said the old man. "Anything to be done this time around?"

"Well —" Uncle Fennimore paused. "Were there any jobs left over from the last time you were here?"

"Yes, sir, there were the paving slabs on the

terrace to straighten out. Mr. Kennington had me
doing a few at a time, in case anybody fell over
them. And then there was the boat, sir, that needed
some attention."

"The boat?"

"For getting over to the island. Letting in the
water, it is. That's got to be seen to."

"Yes, well, we're hardly likely to need that for
the time being. I don't suppose anybody will want
to go to the island. Nothing there to see. So you'd
better attend to the paving slabs this time."

"Right, sir, I'll get on it." He went out, throwing
Carey a little grin as he passed.

"Well, Miranda," said Uncle Fennimore, "how's
the bird?"

47

"He's very well, thank you."

Uncle Fennimore gave a little cough and stroked his overgrown mustache. "I — er — I hear that he's been saying somebody's name."

"He said grace, but I . . ."

"Yes, yes, I know . . . your Aunt Dorothy is very upset about that. I don't suppose he could be taught to say 'Dorothy,' could he?"

Miranda sighed. It was useless trying to explain. "You try," she suggested.

"Do you think he would — I mean, is it possible? Yes, I might try, I suppose." He moved closer to Carey, stared up at him intently, and said in a squeaky voice, "Dorothy — Dor-o-thy."

"Good boy," said Carey. "Hello."

"Hello," said Uncle Fennimore. "Good boy. Dor-o-thy."

"It'll take some time," said Miranda.

"Hee-hee!" squawked Carey. That was something new. He hadn't said that before.

She thought about it. "You'd better come back tomorrow," she said to Uncle Fennimore.

"But I'm making good progress, my dear child. Can't you see how interested he is? Good boy, hello, Dorothy, Dorothy . . ."

"Old hairy nose!" yelled Carey.

For a few moments you could have heard a pin drop, then Uncle Fennimore said, "*Well!*" He turned on Miranda and said, "Did you teach him to say that?" She shook her head. "Then Grandfather Kennington must have taught him to say it to anybody with a mustache. Was there no end to his wickedness?"

"I don't think Grandfather Kennington was wicked," protested Miranda, but all the same, it was puzzling to know why he should have taught the bird to say such a thing. It wasn't like him; he had been such a gentle and courteous old man.

Uncle Fennimore stalked out angrily, and shortly afterward Miranda went down to the lake to look at the boat. It would have been lovely to go for a row on the lake. She wished that Aunt Lucille would agree to stay for a week or two longer, by which time Mr. Perkins would have mended the boat, but there was little hope of that. Aunt Lucille had to be back at work by the end of the month.

She sat down near the spot where she had sat with Grandfather Kennington and thought about

some of the things he had said. The lake wasn't very deep. Many years ago, in order to attract water birds to his garden, he had flooded a shallow depression in the ground, which was fed by a tiny spring. He could walk across to the island, he had told her, if ever he felt so inclined, but a boat had the advantage of keeping his trousers dry.

As she watched, the two swans came gliding around from the far side of the island. They had three cygnets. It was a beautiful sight. How lovely it would be to live here forever, instead of on Walker Street. They didn't even have a garden, and the park across the road was dirty, with litter blowing about everywhere. Sometimes, in the winter evenings, Aunt Lucille would settle down on the rug in front of the fire and talk about her favorite dream. They would save enough money to buy a little cottage in the country, and they would keep chickens, bees, a donkey for herself, and a dog for Miranda. Aunt Lucille would make potpourri and patchwork quilts to sell. Oh, why couldn't it all come true?

Suddenly she wanted to throw her arms around Aunt Lucille, so she scrambled to her feet and went across the meadow toward the front drive. She sat down on the broad stone steps to wait. The bushes were full of birds — thrushes, blackbirds, robins, wrens, and many more she had never seen before. Grandfather Kennington had planted special trees and shrubs to attract them.

She was listening for the sound of Mr. Ryman's car coming along the crunchy gravel driveway when she heard footsteps. A moment later Aunt Lucille appeared. She was not alone.

"Aunt Lucille!" Miranda cried. "What have you done?"

"I've bought a donkey, love. Isn't he sweet?"

"He's beautiful, but what will Uncle Fennimore say?"

"He'll tell me I ought to have more sense, and Aunt Dorothy will tell me I'd no right to do it until we know who's likely to have the house after Carey. Aunt Jane will have hysterics, and Aunt Grace will be *absolutely disgusted*. But I don't care.

I did my shopping and then I went with Jim — with Mr. Ryman — on his rounds. And there was this perfectly adorable little donkey in a nasty little shed, looking so miserable that I couldn't possibly leave him there. So I gave the man ten pounds and — here he is. What shall we call him?"

"Magnus," said Miranda, "after Grandfather Kennington."

They put Magnus in the lower meadow, where he gazed around as if he couldn't believe his luck,

then he rolled over on his back among the buttercups. When they left, he was quietly gorging himself on dandelions.

Miranda gave Aunt Lucille a hug. She was wonderful. Anybody else would have put all sorts of difficulties in the way of bringing the poor creature home, but not Aunt Lucille. She had even used her silk stockings to make a halter. "Let's go and tell them," she giggled.

Chapter 5
The Key

Nothing much happened for a day or two. Uncle Fennimore and Aunt Dorothy were busy sorting out Grandfather Kennington's papers, but everybody knew they were really looking for clues to where the key to the box might be. Aunt Grace was dusting all the books in the library, and as Grandfather Kennington had collected books about birds since he was a little boy, she had an enormous task ahead of her. She seemed to have an idea that the key might be hidden in one of them. Aunt Jane did nothing, as usual, but Cousin Horace was still on his treasure hunt.

Mr. Ryman came twice a day. He said he was coming to check on Carey and Magnus, but Miranda knew he was really coming to see Aunt Lucille. That was all right. Miranda liked the idea that one day the three of them might make up a little family.

Cousin Horace got stuck up a tree. Miranda asked him what he was doing up there and he replied, "You know perfectly well what I'm doing up here, you little fox. You said the key might be in one of the nest boxes."

"I didn't," she said indignantly.

"Well, you implied it. Go and find Perkins. Tell him to bring a ladder. One of the lower branches has cracked, and if I put my weight on it, it will break. Go on — hurry."

Perkins said, "Would that be the young chap who wanted me to dig a hole in the wine cellar? In that case, I'll come when I'm good and ready."

He was good and ready about three-quarters of an hour later, by which time Cousin Horace was furious. Later, he met Miranda on the landing and asked her if she had any more brilliant ideas. "What about?" she asked innocently.

"Anything. I've been watching you these last few days, and you're going around with a grin on your face as if you knew something. Tell me what it is and I'll buy you a bicycle." He looked hard into her face. "You do know something, don't you? Has it got anything to do with that stupid bird?"

It had, and her heart gave a nasty little bump at the thought of Horace finding out. She had to send him off on a false trail again. She said, "When we came to tea with Grandfather Kennington he sat by the lake. He kept chuckling to himself. He said the swans were very aggressive when they were defending their nest, and if ever he had to hide something it wouldn't be a bad idea to hide it there."

"Thanks, Miranda." He grinned. "I won't forget the bicycle."

"Can you swim?" she called after him.

"Swim? Of course I can swim."

"That's all right, then," she said.

It was Magnus who had given her the idea earlier that afternoon. She had been feeding him carrots when he had made a funny snorting sound, and

she had laughingly told him that donkeys were supposed to say "hee-haw." That had led her to think about the way that Carey said "hee-hee." And suddenly she had known. How stupid she had been not to know it before!

After talking with Horace, Miranda hurried off to the conservatory. Nobody was there. As she entered, Carey flew around her head. He had grown accustomed to her now and he seemed to enjoy her visits. Since the wonderful idea had come to her she had tried several times to make Carey say "old hairy nose" again, but he hadn't.

He settled down on his ledge. She looked up at him. "I know what it is you're saying, Carey," she told him. "You're not saying 'hee-hee' at all, but 'key-key.' And if that's so, then it isn't 'old hairy nose' but 'old Carey knows.' That's right, isn't it? Come on, Carey — please. There's no time to lose. You must tell me *what* you know. Where is the key? Key, key, key, key," she repeated in desperation. She held out her hands in a pleading gesture.

That did it. Carey flew down to her, perched on her arm (it was a good thing she had her old brown sweater on), and, to her astonishment and delight, deposited a small silver key in her open hand. He had had it on his ledge all the time! Grandfather Kennington must have trained him to bring it when he held out his hand like that. And, of course, Grandfather Kennington had known that only someone whom Carey trusted would be given the key. That was why he had left the list. Only someone who cared enough to follow the instructions would get the key.

She stroked Carey gently. She really did love him now, and not because he had given her what she wanted, but because he had been the beloved pet of her dear old great-grandfather. She gave him some grapes and hurried out.

The whole family (except Horace, of course) was drinking tea on the terrace. Mr. Ryman was there, too. She said breathlessly, "I want to go into town."

"I'll take you when I go," said Mr. Ryman.

"I want to go *now*."

"That child is behaving very strangely," said Aunt Grace. "Is she feverish?"

"No," shouted Miranda, "I'm not feverish. I just want to go into town. It's important. I must go now."

Mr. Ryman and Aunt Lucille exchanged glances. They stood up. "Very well," they said.

As they went out of the French windows they heard Aunt Dorothy say, "Completely spoiled — gets her own way in everything," but that didn't matter. And as they hurried down the steps toward Mr. Ryman's car they saw Cousin Horace coming across the lawn. He was very wet. His clothes were sticking to him and he was covered with green,

slimy weeds. Miranda couldn't help feeling sorry
for him, but changed her mind a moment later
when he yelled, "You little witch — you knew
there was a hole in the boat, didn't you?"

She couldn't help saying, "Yes, but never
mind — I'll buy you a bicycle to make up for it."

Aunt Lucille was wonderful. She didn't ask a
single question. And all Mr. Ryman asked was,
"Where in town do you want to go?"

"I want to see Mr. Fulton."

They got out of the car in a yard behind an old-fashioned building and went up some dark stairs into Mr. Fulton's office. He looked surprised when he saw them come in and started to talk about Mr. Ryman's bill. "No, no," Mr. Ryman said, "I'm not presenting my bill. It's Miranda who wants to see you."

She didn't say a word. She simply walked up to Mr. Fulton and held out her hand. She had been holding the key tightly ever since Carey had given it to her, and there were red marks all across her palm. There were three distinct gasps all around her. "Carey had it," she said. "He brought it to me."

Mr. Ryman was the first to speak. "Of course!" he said, almost in a whisper. "Parrots can be taught to do the most amazing tricks."

Mr. Fulton unlocked a safe in the corner of the room and took out the box. The key fitted perfectly. Miranda opened the box. Inside was a blue paper that Mr. Fulton began to read silently. When he had finished, he laid it down and handed Miranda another sheet of paper that had been folded inside the blue one. She read it.

My dear Miranda (it said), *I am sure it is you who are reading this letter. I am delighted to leave the accompanying document giving you full title to Kennington Court and all the goods of which I am currently in possession. Mr. Fulton will deal with the legal side of things and all you have to do is to enjoy living*

in your new home. I know you will take care of my dear old friend Carey and my innumerable wild friends out of doors. All my life they have given me joy and companionship, and I believe you have the right spirit to enjoy them, too. Until you are of age, your Aunt Lucille will hold the house in trust for you.

I felt it my bounden duty to give all my relatives an equal chance to inherit my property, and for that purpose I called you all together last year to listen to an old man talk about his abiding passion for wildlife. I have never liked to see birds confined in cages, but I found Carey in a sorry state, imprisoned in a cage in which he could scarcely turn around, and the only way I could give him freedom in our unfavorable climate was to give him the full use of my conservatory.

Be happy, my dear, and forgive an old man who never took the trouble to get to know you better.

Miranda handed the letter to Aunt Lucille, who wept as she read it. Miranda had never seen her cry before. "Don't!" she begged. "You can have another donkey."

Mr. Ryman put his arm around Aunt Lucille's shoulders. "I know the very one," he said. "A poor old thing worn out with giving rides on the beach." Then he turned to Miranda. "And I've heard of another parrot that wants a good home. Do you think . . . ?"

"A companion for Carey!" cried Miranda. "He'll love that!"

Mr. Fulton went back to Kennington Court with them. When he had finished speaking to the family, Aunt Grace said, "Well, child, I hope you realize how very lucky you are to have come into an inheritance like this."

"Luck had nothing to do with it," said Aunt Lucille.

Aunt Dorothy gushed, "Well, I'm sure she won't forget her aunts and uncles, will you, dear? Perhaps there is some little memento we could each have to remember dear Grandfather Kennington by?"

Aunt Jane just sighed.

"I was well on the trail, you know," said Cousin Horace sulkily. "I knew it had something to do with that bird. If *she* hadn't sent me off on that wild goose chase I'd have been onto it before she was."

"I didn't send you on a wild goose chase," Miranda pointed out. "They were swans."

Mr. Fulton looked at Cousin Horace over his spectacles. "The wishes as expressed in Mr. Kennington's final will can only be interpreted as leaving everything to his great-granddaughter, Miranda, regardless of the key to the box, although Mr. Kennington was very confident that it would be Miranda who found it."

There was nothing more to be said. Miranda looked at Aunt Lucille and Mr. Ryman, who were gazing at each other so happily that she knew it wouldn't be long before they were a complete little family — just the three of them, together at Kennington Court.

She crept quietly away to tell Carey all about it.